CH00944899

Beauty and the Beast

RETOLD BY

Samantha Easton

ILLUSTRATED BY

Ruth Sanderson

LEOPARD

This edition published in 1995 by Leopard Books,
20 Vauxhall Bridge Road, London SW1V 2SA

First published in 1992 by Andrews and McMeel

ISBN 0 7529 0111 7

Design: Susan Hood and Mike Hortens
Art Direction: Armand Eisen, Mike Hortens and Julie Phillips
Art Production: Lynn Wine
Production: Julie Miller and Lisa Shadid

Beauty and
the Beast

$\mathcal{T}$here was once a rich merchant who through no fault of his own lost his entire fortune. All he had left was a small house in the country where he and his family would now have to live.

The merchant had three daughters. The youngest was so lovely that everyone called her Beauty.

The merchant had always given his daughters the best of everything, and the two eldest girls were very spoiled. They hated their new home and did nothing but complain about it. Beauty, however, tried to make the best of things.

A year had passed in this way when the merchant received some good news. One of his ships, which he had believed lost, had come into port with all its cargo safe and sound.

Beauty's sisters were overjoyed. They were sure the family would soon be as rich as before. As their father prepared to leave for town, they begged him to bring them back fine silk dresses and jewelled necklaces.

But Beauty asked for nothing.

The merchant noticed her silence. "How about you, Beauty? What would you like?"

"I only wish you to come home safely, Father," the girl replied.

"But there must be something I can bring you," said Beauty's father.

"Very well," she said. "Bring me a rose. None grow here, and I am so fond of them."

So the merchant set off for town. When he arrived he learned that all the cargo had been stolen. There was nothing for him to do but turn around and head home.

When the merchant was only a few miles from home, a terrible storm blew up. The snow fell so heavily that the merchant could not go on. He looked for shelter, but there was none in the forest. He was growing desperate when he spotted a path through the trees. He steered his horse onto it.

As he went down the path the snow cleared and the air grew warmer. Soon the merchant was on a paved road. On either side were orange trees heavy with ripe fruit. "How strange!" he thought. He kept going until he came to a white marble palace.

The gates were open and the palace was entirely lit. The merchant wandered through the rooms, but he could find no one at home. He stopped in a room with a blazing fire. Thinking the fire must have been made for someone who would soon appear, he sat down before it and fell asleep.

The merchant awoke in the morning to find a full breakfast set out for him. He hungrily devoured it, then walked through the palace once again looking for his mysterious host. But he could find no one. Finally he decided to be on his way and went outside to find his horse.

In the garden the merchant saw a rose bush covered with beautiful flowers. "At least, I can bring Beauty her gift," he thought as he plucked one.

Then, a terrible voice above him said, "Thief! Is this how you repay the Beast's kindness? That rose will cost you your life!"

The merchant turned to see a fearsome beast looming over him. "Please forgive me, sir," he cried, falling to his knees. "I only wished to bring a rose to my daughter, Beauty." Then he told the Beast his story.

When the merchant had finished, the Beast said, "Very well, I will spare your life, but one of your daughters must agree to take your place!"

The merchant was horrified. But he accepted the condition, and the Beast let him go still carrying the rose for Beauty.

When the merchant reached home, his daughters eagerly ran to meet him. He gave them the sad news that he was as poor as ever. Then he handed Beauty her rose. "Here is what you asked for," he sighed, "but you cannot imagine what it cost!"

His daughters asked him to explain.

Upon hearing his story, the two older daughters turned on Beauty. "It is all your fault," they said. "You had to ask for a rose, and now look what you have done!"

"I know," Beauty replied. "And so it is only fair that I go to the Beast in my father's place." Her father said he would not allow her to do this, but Beauty stood firm. After a week had passed, Beauty and her father set out for the Beast's palace.

The journey passed quickly. Soon they were walking down the road lined with orange trees. Although Beauty was frightened, she could not help marvelling at the Beast's gardens. They were full of fruit and flowers even though it was winter.

As before the palace was beautifully lit, but there was no one to be seen. Inside, a fire blazed in the same room, and a big meal had been set out. But Beauty and her father were both too upset to eat. After a while, the door opened and in walked the Beast.

The Beast was horrible to look at, but Beauty greeted him politely. He asked her if she had come willingly, and she replied in a steady voice, "Yes, Beast."

The Beast then told the merchant to go home, and he gave him two chests of gold to take with him. Beauty and her father thought they would never see each other again. They embraced and the merchant reluctantly rode away.

Beauty expected the Beast to kill her at once, but he left her alone. When it grew dark, Beauty found herself before a room with her name written above it in gold letters.

The room had a graceful bed and a matching dressing table. The wardrobe was full of lovely gowns. "Surely, the Beast would not give me these things if he meant to kill me," Beauty thought. Then, feeling much better, she fell asleep.

The next morning, Beauty awoke to find breakfast set out for her. All day long she amused herself by wandering through the palace. Sometimes she heard music and voices, but she saw no one.

When evening came Beauty found a delicious supper waiting for her in her room. She was just sitting down to eat, when the Beast knocked at her door. "Beauty," he said softly. "May I please watch you eat?"

Beauty trembled with fear, but she replied bravely, "Yes, Beast."

So the Beast sat beside her, and they spoke of many things. To Beauty's surprise, the Beast was a pleasant companion. But at the end of the meal, the Beast asked, "Do you love me, Beauty? Will you marry me?"

"How can I answer?" Beauty said.

"Tell the truth," replied the Beast.

"Then, no, dear Beast," Beauty replied gently. "I cannot marry you."

"Very well," the Beast said sadly.

Every night the Beast asked Beauty the same question. And even though she refused him, he treated her very kindly.

Soon Beauty began to enjoy living in the palace. Whenever she wished for anything—some embroidery thread or a kitten to keep her company—her wish was granted at once. She also grew very fond of the Beast, who was kind and generous to her. Despite his dreadful appearance, Beauty looked forward to the evenings when he would sit with her.

Yet Beauty missed her family, especially her dear father, and she slowly grew pale and ill from longing. At last, the Beast asked her what was wrong.

"I only wish I could see my family again, dear Beast," Beauty replied.

The Beast sighed. "If you go," he said mournfully, "it will be the death of me!"

"But I will only go for a month," Beauty promised. "Then I will come back and stay with you always."

"Then go," said the Beast. "But be sure to keep your promise or you will find me dead."

The Beast gave Beauty a silver ring and told her to put it on that night and wish she were home. "Tomorrow morning you will be there," the Beast said. "And when you wish to come back to me, put the ring on your finger when you go to bed. Then turn it once, and say, 'I wish to be with my dear Beast again.' By morning you will be here."

That night Beauty filled a trunk with gifts for her father and sisters. Then she put on the ring and wished herself home.

The next morning she was there. Her father was overjoyed. Her sisters pretended they were, too. But secretly they were jealous of Beauty, because the Beast had given her many expensive and beautiful things.

One day Beauty carelessly told them that she had promised the Beast to return in a month. "Let us make her stay longer," said one of her sisters. "Then the Beast may get angry with her and not let her come back."

When it came time for Beauty to go, her sisters burst into tears. "If you leave, we shall die of grief," they wailed. So Beauty stayed one day and then another and another, but she began to worry about the Beast.

One night, Beauty had a terrible dream. In it the Beast appeared before her and said, "Beauty, you broke your promise and now I shall die!"

Terrified, Beauty woke with a start. She placed the ring on her finger, turned it once, and said, "I wish to be back with my dear Beast again."

The next morning Beauty was in the Beast's palace. All day she waited for evening when the Beast would visit her. But evening came, and the Beast did not appear.

Beauty ran through the palace calling his name, to no avail. Next, she ran into the garden. There, she saw the Beast lying very still beneath the rose bushes.

Beauty ran to him. "He is dead," she sobbed, "and it is all because of me!" Just then the Beast's eyes opened. "Oh, Beast!" Beauty cried. "I am so glad you are still alive. I never knew how much I loved you until this moment!"

"Can you really love an ugly beast like myself?" the Beast asked.

"Yes," Beauty replied.

"Will you marry me, Beauty?"

"Yes, I will, dear Beast!"

Then there was a bright flash of light, and the Beast vanished. In his place stood a handsome prince. He told Beauty he had been placed under a spell by a wicked fairy. He was doomed to remain in the form of a hideous beast until some maiden should fall in love with him. Beauty's love had broken the spell, and now the prince wished to marry her.

The prince took Beauty back to the palace and introduced her to his mother and father, who under the wicked fairy's spell had been invisible.

Then Beauty sent for her father and her sisters. She told them of the prince's spell and the coming wedding. And so the marriage of Beauty and her prince was celebrated with great joy, and they lived happily ever after.